Fighting for MY LIfe to Win

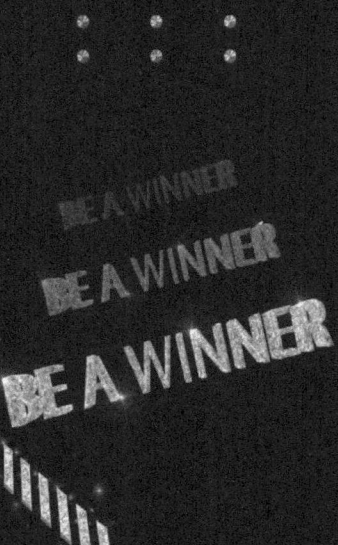

BE A WINNER
BE A WINNER
BE A WINNER

Arshisa Adejiyan

Fighting For My Life To Win

By: Arshisa Adejiyan

Trient Press

3375 S Rainbow Blvd

#81710, SMB 13135

Las Vegas,NV 89180

Ordering Information:

Quantity sales. Special discounts are available on quantity purchases by corporations, associations, and others. For details, contact the publisher at the address above.

Orders by U.S. trade bookstores and wholesalers. Please contact Trient Press: Tel: (775) 996-3844;   or visit www.trientpress.com.

Printed in the United States of America

Publisher's Cataloging-in-Publication data

Barnes, Dr. Carl M.

A title of a book : Resilient Sailing

ISBN

Paperback   : 978-1-953975-31-7

E-book   : 978-1-953975-32-4

Table of Contents

Introduction

This isn't a story of rags to riches. Although I had a challenging environment growing up, I didn't have to drastically alter my economic status in a short span. This isn't a story about that. This is a story of my life, and I prioritize truth. In fact, the only consistent trouble I ever got in was because of the unfiltered truth. I spoke my mind all the time, and I continue to do so in this book. What you'll find here is a beautiful story encompassing the life of a music lover who has the courage to be a great mother despite being in a situation where it can be easy to be neglectful. If you're a single parent or a new parent, this will be very valuable to you. If you're a child who wishes to repair his or her relationship with a parent, this will be helpful. Above all, if you value human connection, you'll love this book regardless of who you are.

The Answer Is Your Childhood

Many people I meet tell me they have problems finding their passion. I believe the answer lies in one's childhood. When we transition from our younger years into adulthood, we end up losing touch with what invigorated us once. This is always, without exception, a bad choice. Why? Because when you chase anything but your calling, you're grasping at straws. I was in a choir in my middle school and my high school. As soon as I graduated, I went straight to music school. This consistency is something I am eternally grateful for because it kept me from losing touch with what fills me with life.

If you have something that fills you with life, please do not lose touch with it. Even if you're doing it for "practical reasons," you are doing something impractical: assuming you'll be happy without the thing you love. If you don't feel particularly passionate about anything, I urge you to go back to your childhood and look for hints. Whatever is supposed to be your calling is likely there.

You'll find it to be an itch. Something you cannot leave the Earth without scratching. For me, that was music. But an interesting twist happened in my story. I went to a music school thinking it was about singing but is focused entirely on audio production. I still did it because it was broadly related to my interests. It may not be the kind of music I did singing for my church, but it was still music.

This brings me to my second lesson: stay broadly close to your interests. Even if you may not be able to monetize them precisely right away, you can still stay within their vicinity so that you have a life with an inlet of passion. If passion doesn't flow through your life, you cannot be passionate towards people. As a mother now, I can truly look back and appreciate the value of having access to my passion because of two reasons.

The first and foremost is that I am a happy person and a positive influence. The second is that I'll never deny my daughter her road to happiness. People who kill dreams are often disconnected from theirs. That's why I wanted to make it a point in my book's first chapter: do not abandon your dreams or steer too far from what you enjoy. Your happiness is your first responsibility.

Children and Passion

Since I'm such an advocate for passion as means to life, I would like to address maturity and what it means to me. I do not like the idea of maturity as the death of childhood. I believe the world is made for children. We're supposed to act right because that's what makes life safer for children. We fall in love and marry only for nature to gift us children. Children are the ultimate lovable beings. You don't need to make a case for this. Strangers walking your child in the street will soften up and smile no matter how tattooed up and tough they look. A child is inherently lovable.

That's why it's interesting to me that so many books about self-love miss the point. You can love yourself more if you keep your inner child alive. You become more lovable by doing it. Period. But keeping your inner child alive doesn't mean being childish. Perhaps if I can clarify this idea, more people would be open to not stifling the existence of their inner child.

Maturity is understanding, whereas childhood is wonder. When you don't understand something, you have a sense of awe about it. Often, when people mature, a lot of things change. My voice changed, and it allowed me to sing in different styles. Refusing to expand one's understanding is childish. On the other hand, expanding your understanding enough to only know how everyday life works and operating within that world will kill your sense of wonder. That's not good either.

But if you keep seeking more knowledge, you'll always have a sense of wonder about something. As of today, I can sing in Latin, Spanish, and Country genres aside from the choir singing that kicked off my introduction to music. I keep learning more, and this keeps my inner childlike wonder alive. More importantly, I engage in things that satisfy my sense of wonder and reinforce my passion.

I found this expansion of knowledge to be unnecessary at certain points, especially when the school made me learn about frequencies and identifying notes by tone. But it eventually helped me realize that things were going to work out. I have learned video editing and have picked up other multimedia manipulation disciplines. It is like one passion opens doors to other territories. And through constant exploration, I've kept my sense of wonder alive. You can do that too if you open the doors to your childhood passion.

My Day-Job Days

I wish I could say that it was all smooth sailing from picking the right school onward. But that's not the truth. I had a few things I needed to improve before I could be functional in that high-pressure environment. IT wasn't high pressure in the general sense of the term but definitely pushed me hard in many ways.

Firstly, I was the only girl in the program, and more importantly, I was shy. Being shy isn't something we choose but deciding to flip our disposition is a choice. I overcame my shyness not as a direct result of my efforts but as their byproduct. I've never focused on changing my personality. Our personalities naturally change across time; that's called growth. But anytime you force growth, you're not just changing yourself. You're changing yourself for others.

Whether you have a dream or a personal interest, you have all the time in the world to pursue it. But the moment you start doing it for others, you have to accomplish things with deadlines. In other words, if you feel like you need to get rich quick, get slim quickly, or get a certain job quickly, you're probably doing it for others.

I am against the idea of losing oneself in service of others' opinions. Singing is perhaps one area where this could be forgiven. After all, it is normalized for singers to chase higher notes because some people think they can't. Other singers switch genres just because their audience believes their style has gotten boring. Singers are encouraged to sing for others.

I decided to sing for myself in a way that's natural to me. Almost every theorist or armchair expert would tell you that's a bad choice. If singing for myself means I'm not going to lean into styles and frequencies that don't sit well with me, most by-the-books people would say I'm not getting into singing like a professional. But what matters is that instead of paralyzing myself with things I don't even enjoy learning, I get to do what most people don't: I get to sing.

Regardless of your interest in singing, the above message applies. You cannot force yourself to chase others' approval. Because if you do that, you abandon your sense of wonder and passion and make people's positive feedback your drug. That's a high you can not perpetually chase because people are, as a matter of fact, never perpetually pleased.

Permission To Write A Book

I do not have a record label deal. I do not make millions from my songs. Both of these are prerequisites for many people before they write their book. Many singers with so much to say aren't writing a book because they don't have a record deal. Then there are signed musicians with even more to say who aren't writing their books because they haven't received a grammy yet. These are all self-imposed restrictions. All accomplishments are subjective, and if you don't notice your own accomplishments, you'll not be able to inspire people to chase their dreams.

I didn't want to get into the music business for fame. I wanted to inspire people with my voice and testimony. I have found so much joy in inspiring my daughter, who is also my biggest hype man and vice-versa. Because I find so much meaning in inspiring people, I thought I would write a book that would help others.

That's when different conditions came into my head. Perhaps I must wait till I break into the music industry in a significant way, then I could write a book about making it in music, I thought. Then I thought about an alternative: I should make a lot of money so I can write a book about how one can earn a lot. These thoughts were swarming in my head, and my daughter could see that I was worried.

"What are you thinking?" she asked with concern in her voice.

"I am thinking about writing a book, but..."

"So you should write a book," she said.

Suddenly the self-imposed objections melted away. I realized that I was thinking with a scarcity mindset. I was acting as if I was going to write only one book in my life. If that were the case, it would make sense to wait till I had more to say. But I figured out that I already have a lot to say.

Bringing this back to the lesson that's in this for you, let's talk about the self-imposed restrictions. Whether you're an artist who believes he has to get certain skills right before starting his practice or a student who feels like he has to get a certain number of certificates before he can start applying for jobs, please realize that all self-imposed restrictions are arbitrary. Figure out what you want and go for it as if you have every right to go for it.

Pause and Detour

From the time in school where I had to sing about the history of Houston to my present practice of free-styling with my daughter, who raps, a lot of things happened. I had to drop out after two years of music school because I got pregnant. Once I returned to school, I went for Medical discipline instead of resuming music. If I were into music for others' sake, I would have given up on music entirely or forced myself to resume music despite my life's circumstances requiring otherwise.

But since I was in music for myself, I knew I had time and would eventually return to it. I have now gone through my educational ladder and am well past my master's degree. Now that I have stable work, I am returning to music and have had a long talk with my daughter about it. She's at an age where she can understand how it will occupy my time, and she supports me.

Balancing family and dreams is such an essential aspect that self-help books overlook. As someone who has authored a self-help book and is currently penning another one, I value both family and dreams. Some personal development is toxic because the idea of picking between family and dreams is emphasized.

I believe one should be able to balance both. Your happiness doesn't exist in a vacuum. I am glad that I put my daughter first and now am in a position to pursue my dreams with her by my side. When I accomplish my goals, one of the key sources of happiness for me will be how proud she is of me. I wouldn't have any of this if I ruined my relationship with my daughter while chasing music.

Make no mistake; it takes a lot of tact and strategy to avoid the clash between personal responsibility and one's pursuit of one's dreams. But it is also something you have to anticipate and avoid. I knew when the time was right to pause the pursuit of my calling so I could be a good mother. Often you might have to put your family first.

It is only when your family demands that you give up on your dreams completely that you have a problem. Because if your family wants you to let go of your dream forever, then it is standing in the way of your happiness. You cannot allow that. Let them be beside you and pause for a reasonable time your pursuits if you have to. But don't ever give up your dreams.

People Don't See Your Past

People do not see your past when they meet you. But that doesn't mean you don't have a past. I'm treated and acknowledged as a calm person in most of my social interactions. No one can tell that my childhood was hell. I was molested as a child. That tends to have adverse effects on one's psyche. While my upbringing was good, my environment wasn't. Since this book is about things that are dear to me, including motherhood, I'll unpack what this should mean for every parent: your home isn't the boundary of the environment.

Your child might have a great home environment, but there's a school environment, there's the street environment, and there's friends' home environment. All of those factor into the totality of what our child is exposed to. Make sure you can tell what good and bad factors are present in each one of these places. You may want to put on the rose-tinted glasses and pretend everything is fine, but that's not the truth unless it is. You can't know that till you look at things objectively and acknowledge the true nature of your child's environment.

My school environment was tough, and things got tougher when I went mute. I had a hard time focusing at school, and with this development, I was left only communicating with gestures. There was no other option but to get into special education classes for a while so accommodations could be made around my communication limits. All my grades were Bs and Cs, but a part of me felt like I was being patronized.

I didn't want to take special accommodations, but the school insisted. So as soon as I was out from under the school's thumb, I vowed never to take any special consideration or accommodation. I excelled without much padding and boosts. In hindsight, I believe the fact that I was forced to take special consideration is what antagonized me against the idea of handouts.

If you push your child or friends to do something by force, they will flip as soon as they can. In my instance, I flipped against taking special support. But if I was forced to do good things, I might have rebelled and done stupid things. Rebellion is human nature. So, please be careful when you're dealing with others. Don't force people to do things that you cannot afford to see them flip on.

Multiple Passions

When we watch movies about people who have achieved something significant, it's positioned as if that's all they did. We are all well-rounded humans and therefore have multiple interests and passions. When I had to pause my pursuit of music education, I didn't give up on passion and go purely for something that would get me money. If you abandon passion like that, it exits from your life. I found another passion that was more financially conducive. That's how I got my medical administration inclination. I knew there would be stable income in it.

There I got to work at the mental health ward, which I loved because of the people I was able to help. Returning to my point about how I want to inspire people with my music, you can see a consistent thread and theme regarding the goodwill of others. Of course, it is not the same kind of help. My music might elevate someone's mood on a rough evening, whereas my work at the mental health ward helped rehabilitate people who had tried to commit suicide. While the methods are quite different, the underlying theme persists. Guess what? It continues to persist with this book. I love to help people.

I urge you to take a deeper look into what really drives you. If you start focusing on that, you'll soon realize that even though there is a single manifestation of your passion, the underlying love can be morphed into many things. If you want to be an actor, for example, you might consider it a passion.

But the underlying love could be to grab attention with a great performance. If you lean into that, you can get that same satisfaction from a variety of things. If you're familiar with Nusret, also known as Salt Bae, because of the way he sprinkles salt on steaks, you know that he went viral for putting on a performance when presenting food to his customers.

There are other ways to satisfy that deeper itch of performance: from theatre to stand-up comedy and even TikTok, do not confine yourself to a single passion. Be open to receiving satisfaction from many passions. The problem with confining yourself to one passion is that it might take a while till that is actualized. Are you not going to enjoy life until you make it as an actor? I don't like that idea, which is why I suggest you stay a performer in every area till you make it as an actor (or whatever your ultimate goal is).

Past Experience
Future Direction

I believe our experience in life is largely relevant to the direction of our future. Some of the most important lessons I've learned have been in the mental health ward environment. As I said earlier, people will judge you by appearance and dismiss your past. They also judge your job on the surface level. For instance, many people think that job is as simple as being a babysitter, but in my mind, I know I'm more than that. I have been a mentor to the individuals who got admitted there. I worked night shifts because I found that time most interesting, but I also learned that no matter what I did to further my interest in any given discipline, I returned to my passion for music.

Of course, being around people who had hit low points or experienced unimaginable horrors makes one realize that one's own life isn't all that bad. That made my time away from my passion for music bearable. When you have to be away from your passion, please find something that you enjoy but make sure you don't opt for something that takes such commitment that you can never find your way back to your passion.

Do not cut yourself off from life and vigor by shutting the doors of return. The things I went through in my childhood could have harmed my mental health so much that I would have been where my patients were. I am so glad that it didn't turn out that way and also because I didn't abandon music to commit to my role in hospital administration. That role spoke to me because of the fact I just mentioned; I could have been one of the people who needed help.

As much as I care about helping people with mental health issues, I cannot help anyone if I don't help myself. I must survive to help others, and to survive is to find one's way back to their passion. We all have meaningful temptations in our lives: things that have significance but aren't our ultimate calling.

Are you engaged in work you like but deep down know isn't your passion? Because if you are, then chances are you have engaged in a meaningful temptation. That can be a problem if you make it a permanent venture. You must find your way back to your grandest dream. You get one life, so you have to aim at your highest ideal.

What Is Family

Family isn't always family. I learned this when I was working at a foster home. Kids from broken families or no families were brought there. I was often called "mother," and I was more of a mother to them than their "real" mothers. One boy was there because he was raped by his family. Yes, people with such experiences manage to have the spirit of a survivor. I witnessed that upfront and realized the significance of family.

We take family for granted. Sometimes we even look at families that have a healthier upfront image and wish we had such a family. But appearances can't be trusted. From appearances, it seemed like Asians don't have mental health problems. That generalization is wrong because in my time working at the mental health ward; I personally witnessed Asians who had mental health problems. Returning to the point about families, though, I need to emphasize that there will be families with better dynamics than yours, and there will be ones that are worse off.

Regardless of the comparison, you must focus on two things: is your dynamic healthy? Are you a contributor? If you're a parent or someone with authority, you can say that you're a contributor to your family dynamic. Then you can ask yourself whether you're fostering a healthy environment for your children or not. Remember, the environment goes beyond just your home. If you're not in a position to change things, at least be honest about whether the dynamic is healthy or not.

Because if you're not honest about the dynamic, you're going to end up getting gaslighted into believing your family is family no matter what. While this may be the case for most people, it isn't necessarily true. I will never help normalize toxic family dynamics no matter what people say or how they judge me. I have seen up close what that does to people.

In fact, I saw fragments of my life play out in each patient I saw. It was truly humbling and also eye-opening. Family is important, but you can get a better understanding of what's healthy by either visiting friends with a healthy family dynamic or discussing your home dynamic with a counselor. Ultimately, the greatest problem with damaged families is that the ones who are affected the worst know the least about how unhealthy things are. It is further reinforced by the idea that family is family no matter what.

It Matters Where You End Up

You may currently be in a situation where it is quite difficult to believe but trust me, one of the most fundamental truths of life is that it doesn't matter where you are; it matters where you end up. You have to end up in a position of advantage. For that, you must be aware of the drawbacks in your development, environment, and upbringing. Usually, it is nearly impossible for us to be objective about these things, but it is essential, and so you have no other option.

I personally have to be honest about the fact that I wasn't all that great at reading. I had to skip that phase in personal development. But because one cannot skip essentials, I had to return to reading education by taking reading classes three to four times. I made the most of it and leveraged it to teach my daughter how to read.

I did not mind the fact that in terms of reading, I wasn't on the same pace as my peers. If you get into comparisons, everything will bother you because, in every dimension, there's going to be someone who has more. There's always someone wealthier, someone younger, and someone healthier. Usually, people who are disengaged from their passion are ones who fixate on comparisons.

If you're content, you won't feel like you need to be better than others at anything. It is the need to feel superior that makes one get into the comparison game. As far as I am concerned, the best comparison one must make is with one's own past. Are you in a better position today than you were yesterday? That is what actually matters because that's what decides whether you end up where you want to be or stay where you are.

The human mind always aims to solve problems. If the problem you're seeking to solve is "I am not better than others," you're accepting by default that you're inferior. This reinforces insecurity. Instead, focus this problem-solving mind on something productive. When it took me too long to write because of my reading issues, I found software to transcribe my words so I could edit them and save time. That's productive problem-solving.

Our education system doesn't encourage this style of thinking, but this is exactly the type of thinking that helps one's status and position in the real world. So, forget about what schools say and embrace creative problem-solving to get to where you want to be.

Functional Perfectionist

I am a perfectionist, and that can be an asset at times and a problem at other times. Some people argue that perfectionism is just an excuse not to put things out into the world. Others suggest the lack of a degree of perfectionism reflects sloppiness. Either way, instead of deciding which school of thought is right, I pondered what would be right for me. I discovered that I did not need to fit into the two boxes provided. I could just as easily be a perfectionist and put out my work. Enter functional perfectionism.

The problem with perfectionism arises from insisting that your first attempt be perfect. But if anyone has been even slightly familiar with art and creativity, they would know that perfection on the first attempt is almost impossible. Therefore it is necessary for one to get past the first attempt.

Functional perfectionism is simply the idea of insisting on a high standard of work but being willing to get there through multiple attempts. In other words, instead of spending years paralyzed in inaction thinking about how to write the perfect book, I can write multiple books with the idea of eventually finding my perfect book. This isn't a novel idea. Almost everyone who performs at the height of any industry, sport, or market subscribes to a form of functional perfectionism.

Even Apple, which is touted as the perfect brand for technology, has launched products with a lot of issues. Most smartphone companies do this. At one point, there were batteries exploring and phones bending in pockets. At other times battery drainage was through the room. Only after rolling things out do they figure what was wrong and scramble to fix it. You must embrace functional perfectionism because, in its absence, you only have sloppiness or amateur perfectionism. Sloppiness doesn't get you anywhere, whereas amateur perfectionism leads you to a life of pain.

No one likes to work forever on one thing trying to make it perfect. The problem with this mode of operation is also that even if you do your best, you're the only observer. This means you're cut off from the feedback of the world. How can anything be perfect without that knowledge? So embrace functional perfectionism and put your work, art, music, and anything else out into the universe. Do not be afraid of it being bad because even if it is, it's not your final work. You'll get another shot.

Don't Be Everything

Do not try to be everything because no one can be everything. Whether you think Michael Jackson was the best singer or Jordan the best basketball player, you know that they weren't both the best writers. They weren't the best furniture markers. I could go on, but you get the point. Anyone who has reached an admirable level of excellence in any domain has done so at the expense of other areas of his life. These areas could be friendships, social life, and even certain hobbies. Once you pick your passion, you're better equipped to make those decisions.

But many people, well before finding their passion, are engulfed in the race towards scattering themselves. I love music, so I know that if I am given a choice between perfecting my ability to write or learning to play the piano, I'll pick the piano. Why? Because someone can be my typist, or I can use an app to transcribe. When I can get help in something I am not too passionate about, I can use my time and energy to excel at what I am passionate about.

Life is a game of stealing time from things you don't feel deeply towards and delegating it to what makes you come alive. IF you empty out the buckets of the mundane and put them into the bucket of life, you'll be a happy person at any given age. On the other hand, if you're one of the poor misguided souls who drains the bucket of passion to fill the buckets of unnecessary responsibility, you'll feel like each day is longer than the previous one.

The question then is: how can one differentiate between the essential buckets and the unnecessary ones. Surely, there must be a criterion that keeps one from making a mistake in something that is as important as discovering what one must delegate and what she must commit to.

Aside from the broad indicators of what fills you with life and what drains you, you can ask yourself a more specific question: what will happen if I don't do this? If the answer is "nothing of consequence," then don't do it. Eliminate it. If the answer is that something bad would happen, your next assumption shouldn't be, "well, then I must do it." Instead, you must ask, "what would happen if someone else did it for me?" From cleaning your clothes to doing the dishes for many things in life, the answer is "things will be fine." If things won't be fine if you personally didn't do something, only then should you focus your own attention towards it.

Pause. Deal. Heal.

Your success may be in your momentum, but your life isn't. Life happens from moment to moment, and you have to have the calmness and composure to pay attention to the moment. Only then can you slow down and heal. I was fixated on my growth and progress with such singular focus that I lost count of everything else. At one point, my professor asked how come I talked about my grandmother all the time but rarely my mother. It was only then that I realized I had some healing to do.

Even right now, as you read this, you may be harboring feelings of resentment that you've not acknowledged. I suggest that you pause and reflect. Ask yourself the three essential questions that reveal resentment.

- Have I constantly done things for someone without receiving gratitude or acknowledgment?
- Have I sacrificed my happiness for someone?
- Has someone wronged me and never apologized?

The worst-case scenario is that the answer to all three questions is "yes" regarding one person. Such a condition would definitely lead to uncontrollable resentment. You definitely need to take time away from the fast-paced high-speed life in order to truly heal. You must forgive the other party in the process. I know this might not sound beneficial at first. Still, it is for your sake more than theirs.

Forgiving others doesn't free them of anything; it frees you of the burden of carrying a grudge. As mentioned earlier, your focus and your energy are important. Both of these are wasted keeping track of who you're angry at and for what reason. Forgive and move on. Many people are wary of the idea of forgiving because they think it entails welcoming the person back into your life. That's not the case. Your forgiveness doesn't entitle someone to anything other than a lack of animosity.

If someone was your best friend and he betrayed your trust, forgiving him doesn't mean you have to give him the same degree of trust as before.

35

In fact, you can move on and never even meet again and still have no grudge. As long as you go to bed not wishing them harm, you're doing your part in clearing your heart of resentment.

Only in the absence of resentment can healing take place. I got to pause and reflect. With my church and my belief system helping me, I got to heal, and I am better off for it. I wish the same for you. Therefore, I emphasize the importance of forgiving for your own sake and moving forward with a clean heart.

Self-Mentoring 101

Being your own mentor is like playing life as an advanced game. Some of us become our own mentors because we don't have any other option. Others become self-mentored because they lose trust in the people around them. I was taken advantage of in my childhood, and I don't want that to repeat again. Now, there's more at stake, and it leaves no room for slacking. This chapter is for people who find themselves in a similar situation. If you lack access to the right mentor or simply cannot build enough faith in people to rely on others, you'll learn here how you can manage your personal progress without a mentor figure.

I had to personally manage my own healing process by sitting myself in my church. There are other areas of life, too, where I'm self-taught and thoroughly researched. This brings me to the first pillar of self-managed personal progress: learn from authoritative sources. I don't find it easy to trust someone who says he or she can fix all my problems. But if there's a resource online that has proven to help a fair number of people, I find it worthy of a read.

We aren't all readers or video viewers. There are different modes of learning. Some of us love to read books. Others listen to audio-books and podcasts. There's a lot of information in video format, and experimental learners like to learn by getting their hands on something. Knowing your personal learning style helps you narrow your search for resources to glean information from.

The next step is to filter by agenda. Yes, no matter how helpful someone might seem, you have to remember that everyone has an agenda. It isn't even wrong to have an agenda. It is, however, problematic if you're unaware of someone's agenda and are playing into it without realizing it. There's no such thing as free lunch.

Knowing this and strategizing accordingly allows you to be ten steps ahead. Take control of the agenda and make it work for your benefit as well as the benefit of the platform you're using. I like to follow the money to figure out the agenda. If I'm taking a course or getting an online education, I prefer a platform that seeks subscriptions. Since they're not looking for a one-time fee, they're clearly interested in providing long-term value. Ultimately, knowing what you want to learn and what format you best learn in can help you figure out the resource of your choice. Find your resource and make sure you're okay with its backers' agenda and you're ready to excel without a mentor.

Clinging Causes Pain

Friendships and relationships are tricky not just because people can be unreliable and change over time but also because you decide when you're younger whom you would like to be with when you're older. If you've formed these bonds out of geographic convenience or even as a result of shared trauma, things get even more complicated.

When I took a deep dive into my personal history and self-healed the wounds that I had carried and protected for a long time, I began to notice how most of these were due to the things I clung to that did not serve me. Every time I insisted on keeping things in my life that no longer had any business being there, I was disappointed or hurt. No one wants to admit this, but I realized that my marriage was one of those things.

My marriage wasn't a mistake because saying that would imply that I didn't like any part of it. Even the parts I wasn't so enthusiastic about served as lessons. So, I do not consider my marriage an error, but I believe that it was a choice made by my younger self when she wasn't in the clearest state. The tragedy of social decisions is that we make them for our future selves without realizing what our future selves will become.

What's important, though, is that we don't insist on sticking by those decisions when we realize that we need things changed. You are not a slave to your younger, more naive, and more wounded self. Your past serves you, not the other way around. It took a lot of courage to confront this reality regarding my marriage. For some, it takes a lot more strength to realize similar things about their friends.

But the fact remains that it is entirely impossible for a hundred percent of our decisions to be accurate. So, when it comes to the friends and connections we have made in our childhood and youth, we can only hope that the closest ones and the ones most important to us don't turn out to be ill-fitting in our later years. If they do, a lot of times, people will spend the rest of their lives in denial.

Denial is what keeps the pain dormant yet perpetually present. Whenever given a choice between slow-burning, ever-present pain and a quick flash of apparent pain, I always opt for ripping off the band-aid.

Is Your Partner Your Ally

In the previous chapter, I laid the foundation for how our decisions from when we're younger can prove to be ill-fitting when we mature. Here, I will get more personal and, in the process, help many people dealing with similar issues: a partner with a different agenda. Whether you're married, engaged, dating, or single, you need to read this and internalize the importance of matching values.

Your partner has to move at the same pace as you. If you flip perspectives, one can say that you must move at the same pace as your partner. One of you might be slower, and that's the person who is holding both of you back. While this may not be objectively wrong, it harms the one with higher drive. So the question you have to ask yourself is whether you're a high-drive individual or a low-contentment individual. The low-contentment types need an average amount of wealth and rote stability to be happy. This mode of being isn't wrong, but it is wrong for the high-drive person to be partners with a low-contentment individual.

Regardless of which mode is dominant in your operations, you need to know which one you identify with. If you have ambitions that cannot be fulfilled with the average income in your country, you're a high-drive person. If you find perpetual upward mobility in any domain (skill, visibility, or finances) thrilling, you're a high-drive person. On the other hand, if you like to create routines and live within them and the thing that upsets you the most is a disruption to that routine, you're a low-contentment person.

I am a high-drive person because I cannot be happy with a routine of living in a 2-story home with a car and a white-picket-fence while going to a draining job only to return home and repeat the whole thing the next day. I wouldn't be happy in such a circuit even if the job I was doing involved mental health ward administration, which I kind of like.

I realized my husband did not see things the same way. No one wants to admit this in a marriage, so it was a tough pill to swallow. The lesson for most people, though, is to sort this out before. If you're looking for a partner, make sure you're aware of their modality and are compatible with it. Otherwise, you'll both go on the same treasure hunt looking for different treasures. One will be disappointed.

Room To Change or Door To Leave

Now that we have out of the way the filter through which younger people can run potential matches to find the more compatible ones, we have to consider the couples who find out they're not the right modality match a few years into their marriage. I want to dedicate a whole chapter to this because I was in this situation, and the experience was quite draining.

The first thing you must realize is that one of the two modalities has room for change. The person who is content with less can humor the one who is interested in more. The other way around doesn't work as much. Still, the one who isn't as driven must be asked. If you're the most driven in the marriage or the relationship, you must ask your partner if they can support your dreams.

If their answer is that they cannot, or they come up with an excuse as to why they cannot, you know you're incompatible. If they say they'll try, you can go with the three-strikes policy. I implemented this policy in my life just to see if my partner could avoid holding me back. When it became obvious that he could not help himself but hinder my progress, I had to make the tough decision.

That brings me to the options part. Once your partner positions himself as an obstacle in your path, you have two options. You can either decide that he or she is the destination and stop exactly where he appears, or insist on your dreams and move on beyond them. One of these choices will be more immediately painful. That much is evident.

Leaving your partner will hurt more in the short term because there's a past and shared emotional connection. Often it is not even an emotional connection that's present but one that used to exist before. It is amazing how long people will stick around with partners for the sake of who they used to be. But if you choose that nostalgia or shared past and decide to prioritize your partner while they refuse to prioritize your dreams, you'll end up hurting more in the long term.

Your partner, because of their modality, can't even imagine what you're sacrificing to be with them. As a result, there will be no acknowledgment or gratitude. At the same time, you'll live without access to your dreams and passion, but with the person who you'll see as the reason, you're not happy. It might hurt, but letting go is right.

Can You Afford To Walk Away

Whether you're in the music business, general business, or a marriage, you must realize that the weight of all decision-making lies on what you can afford to walk away from. When you walk away is dictated quite directly by what you value more. Since 2016, even as a student, I have had trouble with my partner. I asked God for help through it all. But things stayed the same all the way to 2019. In this period, I had finished school, moved twice between Houston and Irving Texas, and realized that despite telling my husband things needed to change, I had seen no real change.

I walked away not even because of my dreams but because of how much I value peace. His hindrance caused friction and tension between us, and I couldn't take it anymore. But I want to move this from the context of marriage to a broader context. Marriage is a deal, a contract, and so is every other relationship, including one between customers and brands.

It is then important to know what one values. Know what you prioritize the most and also figure out what the other party values a lot. That's what is essential. If my husband knew I valued peace, he would have managed to retain me by making our relationship a peaceful environment. But he valued comfort more and therefore decided to keep things the same way.

In business deals, you must know what you're willing to walk away from. This will give you the power of self-knowledge, which is crucial. More importantly, you must know if the other party is willing to walk away. The loser is always the person who cannot afford to walk away. If you inherently assume the position of someone who isn't willing to walk away, you cannot truly negotiate.

Many people overblow how much they need a certain job or even a spouse and, as a result, strip their own ability to walk away. At that point, their partner has free reign over how they want to be in the relationship. Whether it's a husband who won't stop cheating or an employer who keeps humiliating the employee, the harm happens only when one party decides they cannot walk away.

My conclusion here is that your dignity and your peace are two intangible things but by all means valuable enough to be prioritized over everything else. You should be willing to walk away when they're attacked.

The Pain and Gain

Walking away from a partner can be painful and it was indeed painful for me. I had to self-heal, and I did it with music and laughter. That's why I want to share music with the world. I have seen upfront how powerful it can be. I did not rely on lawyers for my divorce and did everything myself. To distract myself from the pain, I would often browse TikTok. It was quite interesting how music had found its way to me via the app.

It was low-maintenance access to music and doing things with music. I started doing duets on TikTok. It is unlikely that my readers don't know what a duet is, but if you're unfamiliar with TikTok, let me explain. A duet is the app's in-built feature that allows you to make reaction videos of sorts to other TikToks. I received encouragement from people's reactions.

People's reactions have always been a barometer considered. The world's feedback can show where you're doing something that has the potential to 'pop.' I started my "The Spontaneous Queen" brand in 2017 because of external encouragement. It wasn't the only reason, but people's reactions and support definitely played a role in making me see that this could resonate with them.

The greater reason was that I wanted to return to music and dance. I used to dance as a child but was left with very little time as an adult. However, when I was giving so much of my time and myself to my job, I found it unfair to my passion. The last straw was when my manager took it personally that I was helping her learn. Yes, not only was my manager incompetent, but she was also too insecure to receive help in the matter.

I realized that it wasn't worth it to put all my energy into a day job where the manager hated me for no valid reason. The Spontaneous Queen started out as a wellness company. Since I found dance and music to be therapeutic, it was a way for me to extend the gift of healing and positivity to the world.

Whenever you're starting a business, it is essential to place its foundation in something you find personally valuable. When you value your service, you can sell it with authenticity. You no longer feel like you need to use "Sales tactics"; it becomes as natural as convincing your friends that a movie is good.

Environments and Well-Being

The previous chapters have focused on one-on-one relationships and how they can adversely impact your performance. Now we'll explore the effects of an environment as a whole on one's psychological wellbeing. This could be anything from a classroom environment to a workplace setting.

I had PTSD from my unhealthy job environment, and I carried that baggage into the new environment. This could happen to you, so make sure whenever you leave a job, you reflect on the experience and carry out an emotional audit. What is an emotional audit? An emotional audit takes account of whether one's emotional needs were met in an environment. It's a way to stabilize your expectations.

For example, if a workplace is so toxic that yelling and getting yelled at is the norm, someone might exit the environment and enter another office with the expectation to be yelled at or to be given a free pass for yelling. This would most definitely upset people in the new office and lead to disappointment for both parties. In other words, an emotional audit is essential. It is also something that I did not do.

As a result, I got unfairly hesitant regarding my applications. I did not apply for project management roles because I had started associating the position with workplace politics. I know I'm good at the job because I have a history of superior performance. But I also have a history of not being very receptive to workplace politics. For me, performance matters, and I cannot handle coddling a manager who knows less than me. If I don't know something and a junior is willing to help me, I'm grateful. The least I expect from a senior when I do the same is not to get angry.

The problem, however, isn't that all project management jobs are like this. It is that I have started expecting them to be this way because of my experiences. The lesson for you here is that without a timely emotional audit, you have no way of knowing whether you're sabotaging yourself in similar ways.

In order to audit your experience, you have to rate the environment (workplace, home, college dorm, etc.) on a scale of one to ten for each of the following categories.

- Value-match: Do your personal values match with the values that seem to run the place?
- Social cohesion: How well do you get along with the majority of the people in the environment?
- Dignity: How protective is the place for your personal dignity?

Emotional Audit

The emotional audit helps you rate your previous environment and be aware of the abnormalities in it. This means when you enter a new environment, you can expect it to be less extreme in those areas. I personally like this idea as it keeps me from shutting off from the world and being open to new experiences. While my home environment during my marriage wasn't as supportive, I still managed to write a self-help book which subsequently resulted in an invitation.

I was invited to speak at a women's conference and thankfully didn't take the expectation of my previous workplace environment or my married life home environment there. I went there with an open mind. It was my first time going by plane without anyone, or so I thought. My mother tagged along, which I didn't mind. The experience helped transform me in one fundamental way: I added public speaking to my skill set.

Public speaking is an important skill, and you never know when it can become professional speaking. The difference between public speaking and professional speaking is that professionals get paid. I am personally a semi-professional speaker. I speak in a professional capacity from time to time but am focusing my core capabilities on building my business.

The reason I put my brand first is that its name came to me through divine inspiration. I was given the name "The Spontaneous Queen" by God, and therefore I take it as my mission to establish the business. One of its flagship services is to teach people to dance their lives into order. When life gets messy, things get chaotic. In the period of one's life where one seeks order, dance and music can help calm the mind.

The human mind is more powerful than we can imagine. With a calm mind, one can operate as an organizing machine. Once you organize things and put everything where it is supposed to be, you find yourself strategizing instead of over-thinking, and the right strategy makes all the difference.

My clients have figured out new career paths, job interests, and even ways to make their relationships work after learning to calm their minds through dance and music. I found my happy place this way, too, and have realized that music is a universal passion even for people who don't know they're passionate about it. Granting one access to this passion in an organized form such as dance allows for a wholesome process to occur that opens previously unopened doors of possibility.

Success Is A Tightrope Walk

Success is a tightrope walk, not a bus stop. Too many people have consumed the idea that success is something they can reach piggybacking off a mentor or a guru. I don't believe that. That's something sold through marketing, and whenever someone buys that idea, he or she spends money instead of making money. Others can help you spend your money, but no one can help you make money unless you're willing to do the work.

I could say that my dance company is the cure all for failures in life. I could promise you that through my services you'll become the next millionaire, but I don't. The reason is simply that I prefer the truth. Trust us; I can simply help you declutter and make sense of things. From there onwards, you need to abide by the universal principles of success to make things work. You cannot bypass logic and hope for things to work out for you by playing out in an illogical manner.

For example, I want to sing, and my asthma prevents me from being able to do that if I eat cheese. Eating cheese can lead to rapid mucus buildup, which doesn't exactly accentuate one's singing voice. My point is if I continue eating cheese, no guru in the world will improve my singing ability. Similar conditions apply to you. You have to eat right to be successful at staying fit. You have to have the right mindset and spending practices to be an entrepreneur. Whatever you pick as your definition of success comes with its inbuilt principles.

You can never be greater than the principles. If your ego convinces you to abandon the logical principles of success, you will end up with a problem. I don't want my child to go through that, so I've stopped treating her as a child. I talk to her as a future entrepreneur. My belief is that our desired goals are all in our respective vaults. We get access to them in proportion to how well we can believe in them.

My current treatment of my daughter is setting her up to be able to access her vault more. I am educating her in a way that puts her ten steps ahead of her peers. You need to this with everyone. Talk to people as if they're great and watch them become great. It might seem like you're serving them, but ultimately, the seeds you plant come back to serve you.

Humanity Matters

Workplaces don't need to be robotic. In fact, workplaces have to be human to keep the best talent from falling through the cracks. One of the key principles of my life is to use my experience to help others. This is a broad ideal that will lead to a string of companies with very specific service propositions. One of the businesses I am contemplating is a workplace policy management service. The challenge with such a business is that those who need it the most are in the strongest denial.

They don't believe they need it, which makes it perfect for them. Usually, people only realize they need to change things in the workplace only after the business is about to collapse or the best people leave. Even then, some owners end up blaming "competitors" for "Stealing" their "best people." I don't buy that for a second. Why would your best people leave if they were treated like the best people? My service will help depoliticize the work environment using emotional audit feedback from an aggregate of employees.

This feedback will reflect employees personally as well as the workplace as a whole. If, for example, a personal integrity score is low across a majority of the employees, one can tell that the workplace isn't conducive to positive values. On the other hand, if the value-match isn't occurring as often in one environment, one can tell that the employees within that team just do not fit in the culture. It is never one party's fault entirely. That's where the hard truth surfaces: you have to be willing to let go of people. If people resign from your company, you're wrong.

You're either wrong for mistreating them or for not realizing that they weren't the right fit. People don't leave the day they resign; they mentally resign a month prior and are collecting a paycheck. You have to be able to spot those people and either fire them before or get them back in the fold by improving your workplace culture.

As you can imagine, this is no easy feat, and I am putting a lot of my project management experience into building processes to improve mismatch detection, figure out the messy areas of a work environment, and ultimately coming up with a script through which employers can run their work process and fix it. I expect to launch this business at a later date because I still have to figure out how to get the employers who need the service to realize they need it.

Awareness Is Essential

I concluded the last chapter with a challenge. Not a challenge to you, the reader but a challenge that I am facing in setting up one of my businesses. Being aware of the obstacles to expect is so important because when your path is hindered by it, you don't take it personally or overblow it in your head. You realize that it is something you knew was coming all along and then you do what's most important. You keep going.

I'm proud of a number of my accomplishments, and in each one, there's a theme of knowing the obstacles beforehand. When I was with my husband and was contemplating leaving, I knew it would be hard and that it would hurt not to be with him. I wasn't, then, scared when the first pang of loneliness and pain hit and I kept going.

I used to let people walk all over me, and at one point, I realized that I had a daughter whom I want to teach how to stand up for herself. Children don't learn by listening to what you're saying. They learn by following your example. I had to strengthen my backbone and stand up for myself. When I decided that, I knew that people would distance themselves, and those who had come to expect no resistance from me would be disappointed. When it happened, I didn't think anything of it. It was expected, after all, so I kept going.

This isn't even something I picked up as a mature adult. Even in school, I tried to audition for Derby Dolls but didn't make it. I had apparently missed one step. The rules seemed to have gotten more strict because a black girl was auditioning. But I expected this as I had seen the proportions of black people in the dance group. So I did not wallow in self-pity or take it as a reflection of my performance. I kept going.

I went to the counselor and got permission to start my own group where race and gender did not matter. All throughout those years, I had my own group, and we had our own numbers. Above all, it was something I achieved because I could strategize according to the obstacles I anticipated.

Your lesson here is to start expecting the worst. Yes, optimism is good but unchallenged optimism leads to sudden pessimism the moment things don't go your way. True optimism is to expect the worst and still know you'll make it despite the greatest challenges.

Avenues Of Impact

There are multiple avenues of impact for your future self. If you consider them all, you can leave behind a legacy. But for that to work out, you need to be intentional about the process. In this chapter, I will use my future self as a case study, and it'll be interesting for both my readers and me to look back on this and realize how much of it gets actualized. At the same time, it will serve as motivation for me to follow through with what I have said.

The first step in maximizing one's impact is to pick one thing to focus one's energy on. Too many people try to be a million different things and obviously fail to become great at any particular thing. I've chosen singing because of the reasons outlined throughout this book. The next step of the process is to imagine yourself at the heights of fame.

While it might not be the right level of humility for the optics, the exercise demands that I imagine myself in place of Beyonce, Rihanna, and Madonna. If you're interested in Basketball, you'd need to picture yourself as a Jordan or a Lebron. Next, you'll need to map out all the different methods of impact accessible to you. I can see that Rihanna, Beyonce, and Madonna aren't just singers.

They're influencers and they're not influencers in the sense that they have large followings. They're influencers because they are true movers and shakers. The impact culture at large, and when they say something, people listen. So one way I can leave an impact as a singer is by using my voice. Then, there's money. The top singers make a lot of money and donate millions to charities and causes they believe in. This brings us to the third and final step of this exercise: picking a cause.

I want to establish an environment where children can open up and feel safe. So many kids from broken families are put in ill-managed environments where they're still molested and abused. Organizations with a lot of money can't appropriate funds to curb this or do anything to better the lives of these kids. This cause speaks so personally to me that I can commit to it without second-guessing anything. All in all, it's about picking a lane, realizing different ways the leaders in that lane leave an impact, and figuring out which cause you may want to further once you're at the top. Then all you have to do is reach the top.

Moving Away And Moving Forward

Since we're nearing the end of my book, I want to get a chapter on surviving solo out of the way. While the overall book is about passion, you will find people moving away from you once you commit to the passions and the causes that are dear to your heart. It might be scary at first. Believe me; no one understands that better than me. I used to be so attached to people because I am a people person and didn't exactly grow up in a metropolitan concrete jungle. As a consequence, I saw the same people over and over and built a sort of bond with them.

When people started to get busy with their lives or developed different values and distanced themselves from me, I realized that I had to learn how to survive solo. If you're in the same town you've always been in, it is quite easy. You just have to find things you like to do that do not require people's presence. This is naturally easier for introverts, but extroverts can find online socializing somewhat gratifying. But when you move places, you have to be on a different level of survivor mode altogether.

I moved to Houston alone, and though my mother volunteered to tag along, I had to refuse. I was too independent to have that sort of authority looming over me. It would be like the worst of both worlds because I would move and leave everything behind yet not enjoy the freedom that comes with such a move. So I would essentially be throwing all the good of the place I just left while taking on the biggest drawback of being there: the weight of expectations and the presence of dictation.

Moving solo, I had to learn to enjoy my own company. This part is truly important because if you depend on people for your happiness, they control whether you get to be happy or not. I do not want to give people that control. In fact, I detach emotions from words just so no one can hurt my deliberate use of harsh language. This might not be everyone's cup of tea but to learn to be happy in one's own company is essential for everyone.

Ultimately, solo survival is about being resourceful and enjoying one's own company. Once you can do that, other people's presence becomes optional. That's where you're in the true position to decide whether you want to hang out with someone or not.

Attachment and Detachment

When you attach yourself to a passion, you must detach from some people. The solo survival chapter teaches you how to survive in people's absence, but how can one let go of people in the first place? It's tough to move on, especially if you have high levels of empathy. Having high levels of empathy by definition implies that you care more than the average person. In fact, the people you're removing from your life might not even care that you're detracting your presence from their surroundings. You might be the one most affected, emotionally, by the decision. Still, the decision is essential at a certain point.

Many theories have been put forth regarding the subject. The replacement hypothesis suggests that the person you're attached to is serving a specific need. As long as you can replace that need, it gets easier to remove the person in question from your social circle. I do not agree with this because it assumes that everyone seeks connections, consciously or unconsciously, with a goal in mind. That might be true for some people, even most people, but it isn't true for everyone.

Some of us are people pleasers, people's people, and we derive pleasure from helping and connecting without expectations. You as a reader might resonate with this because it is unlikely that someone self-interested with little interest in others would make it this far into a book that is mostly about me. If replacement theory isn't on point, perhaps the fading theory is?

Fading theory suggests that gradually reducing the time you spend with someone might be the answer to the emotional attachment problem. I believe this theory works for some relationships but not all. There are certain relationships that are built with the explicit expectation of time-consuming presence. While you can fade away a friend's presence like a radio's volume knob, you can't do the same with your employer or your wife. You're expected, just by virtue of being an employee or a husband, respectively, to be around them for a specific amount of time.

In my estimation, the best way to let go of people is to let go of people. While no one is perfect at getting over the emotional pain of moving away from people, we don't want to be perfect in this regard as that would require apathy. Having empathy means it'll hurt when you let go. But the only way to let go is to let go.

Control Your Wants

As the final chapter of this book, this page carries a lot of significance and weight. I don't want to leave you with the idea that isn't worthy of remembering. So, here's the idea worth pondering: you must want what you get. The common assumption is that you must get what you want, but if you don't take control of what you want, wants will be imposed upon you. Do you want the fancy car, or is it the want imposed on you by a society where people with fancy cars are respected? If we explore this question, we'll realize that very few of our desires are actually our own.

The perfect example of getting intentional about one's wants comes from the fact that I was never told that the man raising me wasn't my father. Still, by being observative and seeing a facial-feature mismatch, I could tell that the man wasn't my biological father. Only upon realizing this did I begin to want a meeting with my father.

It was manifested through the most curious set of events in 2016. This included my aunt admitting my theory was right, giving me my father's number, and there eventually being a DNA test. All of that happened only because I wanted to meet my father. I could have gone my whole life without cultivating that want had it not entered my knowledge that my actual father isn't the one raising me. How's this relevant to you?

Well, people cannot get what you're selling without wanting it. Regardless of whether you're a business owner or just want to sell yourself as an employee or even a podcaster, you need to persuade people to want what you're putting out there. For that, you must penetrate their knowledge. This isn't even for your sake exclusively. It's for their sake as well. Without the desire to meet my biological father, I wouldn't have met him, and the idea of my first book, his idea, wouldn't have actualized. Guess what? Without my first book, there would be no second book either.

All in all, you have this book because I got to learn about something that fueled a certain desire. Do the same favor to others by expanding their knowledge. The more they learn about you, the better positioned they are to desire what you have to offer. The more people get what you're selling, the more doors open up for them.

Conclusion

Thank you for indulging me and reading this book through to the end. I will leave you with a few words on passion, bringing this book full circle. I believe that one's passion is the gateway to their respective life force. The greatest tests in life then aren't tests of faith, patience, or financial acumen. Our greatest test is a singular one: whether we give up on our passions or we hold them dear, despite it seeming illogical, impractical, and impossible. Whether you've put your passion on a hiatus or contemplated giving it up, I urge you to return to it because the essence of your life is in it. If reading this book only persuades you to indulge in what invigorates you for five minutes a day, I consider my job done. Live well, live with passion.

About The Author

ArShisa Adejiyan is a well-rounded leader, speaker, arthur, divine healer, recording artist with a background in business   healthcare administration. She is a master's degree holder with a big heart to help her community. ArShisa enjoys mentoring children and women and giving back to organizations. She has experience in church sectors where she has an certification in call to accountability. ArShisa is set out to speak and empower people all over globally.

Connect With Me

Our conversation does not end here!

Join my online communities and get more from me and my network on a regular basis:

Website: www.Spontaneousqueen.com
Facebook: @SpontaneousKingzandQueenz
Manifest Your Dream Life
www.facebook.com/groups/569939480826060/?ref=share
Instagram: @spontaneousqueen
Business Number: 281-806-5366

Cozy Corner Publishing

A publication of Cozy Corner Publishing
Galveston, TX
©2021 by Cozy Corner Publishing

CPSIA information can be obtained
at www.ICGtesting.com
Printed in the USA
LVHW101123240822
726691LV00004B/237